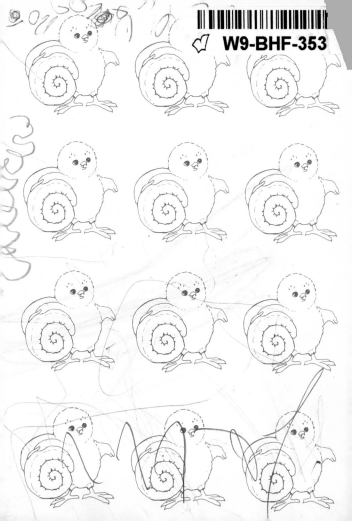

W9-BHF-353

LITTLE OWL
and the Tree House

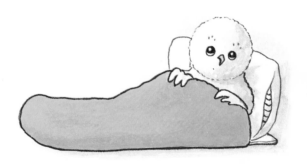

Constance Boyle

Woodbury, New York · London · Toronto · Sydney

First U.S. edition published in 1985
by Barron's Educational Series, Inc.

© Constance Boyle 1985

This book has been designed and produced by
Aurum Press Limited,
33 Museum Street, London WC1A 1LD, England.

All inquiries should be addressed to:
Barron's Educational Series, Inc.
113 Crossways Park Drive
Woodbury, New York 11797

International Standard Book No. 0-8120-5677-9
Library of Congress Catalog Card No. 85-9206

PRINTED IN BELGIUM

5 4 3   9 8 7 6 5 4 3 2 1

When Little Owl was small, his brother Olly had a tree house.

It was in a tree on
the lawn, in front
of their house.
Olly and his
friends had made it
themselves.
It was very high
up.
Little Owl had
never been up
there—

Olly had invited
him, but he
couldn't manage
the rope ladder.

Little Owl couldn't understand why. It looked so easy.

One day, Little Owl discovered that he could climb a twisty little tree in the garden.

The same day, a new freezer arrived in a
huge cardboard box.
As Little Owl looked at it, he had an
idea.

"Can I have the box?" asked Little Owl
when the freezer had been taken out.
"Yes, if you want it," replied his mother,
looking surprised. The box was very
heavy. He could only just manage to
push it along.

Once outside, the box slid down the back steps all by itself. Then Daddy came from the back yard to help.

With a bit of a struggle, Little Owl and
Daddy jammed the box into the twisty
tree, so that the box was wedged quite
firmly.

Then Daddy
got a saw and
cut out a window
and a door.

"It's VERY tough cardboard," he said.

After they had put some thick plastic sheeting over the top, to keep the rain out, the tree house was finished.

Little Owl went inside. At last he had a tree house of his own!

Mommy and Olly came out into the garden. They were very surprised to find a tree house, and Little Owl looking out the window.

"Can Henrietta come to tea?" asked
Little Owl.
"Of course," said his mother. "She
would like to see your tree house."

Henrietta came
the next
afternoon, with
Aunt Willow.

Henrietta loved the tree house, and they had tea there.

After tea, Little Owl's mother found them a piece of carpet and some material that they could cut up for curtains.

They were busy at work when they heard some odd bumping noises on the roof.

Olly's face appeared at the window. "Wow!" he cried. "We don't have carpets and curtains in OUR tree house!"

They scrambled down, and went into the house.

"Is Henrietta staying the night in Little Owl's tree house?" demanded Olly.

Aunt Willow looked doubtful.

"It's extremely strong," said Mommy. "I'm sure it's quite safe."

"Well, all right then," said Aunt Willow, laughing. "What an adventure, Henrietta!"

Little Owl and Henrietta just fit
comfortably into the little tree house.
"I like it here," said Henrietta.
"It's cozy and not too high up."

"Well, we know you two enjoyed yourselves," said Daddy at breakfast next morning. "We could hear you giggling half the night!"

"It was fun!" said Henrietta. "We saw the stars when it got dark."

Henrietta had to go home that afternoon, but she promised to come again soon so she could play in Little Owl's tree house.

That night, Little
Owl took his
sleeping bag out to
the tree house
again.

His mother came to say goodnight.
"Are you sure you'll be all right by
yourself?" she asked.
Little Owl nodded.
But he did feel a
bit lonely when she
had gone.

In the middle of the night he woke up
feeling cold.
The wind was blowing, and the rain was
coming in through the window.

Little Owl pulled the sleeping bag up
around his ears and hoped the rain
would stop.

There was a sudden gust of wind, and a ripping noise as the plastic sheeting was torn off the roof. Little Owl heard it flapping away in the dark.

The rain started to pour in and soon the water was quite deep.

Little Owl struggled out of his sleeping bag. When he stood up, the floor felt strange and soft. The cardboard was soaked through.

Suddenly, the tree house collapsed, and
Little Owl was swept out of the tree on a
wave of water.

As he picked himself up, the lights in the house started to go on, and a moment later Daddy came running from the house.

"Are you all right?" he cried.
"Whatever happened to the tree house? Good heavens! You're soaked!"

Daddy picked up
Little Owl and ran
back through the
rain to the house.
Everyone was up.

His mother dried
him with a big
towel, and sat him
in a chair near the
fire.

"Gosh, you are lucky," said Olly enviously. "I'VE never been washed out of a tree house! You must have nearly drowned! Pity about the tree house, though," he added.

Little Owl was
soon put to bed
with a hot drink.
Teddy was there
already.

"I'm sorry about the tree house, Chick,"
said Mommy. "It must have been scary
for you."

Little Owl was very tired. It was nice
to be back in his own cozy little bed.
But perhaps he would make himself a
proper tree house, like Olly's . . .
One day, when he was bigger . . .